W9-BUO-411

School-Tripped

Also by Jennifer L. Holm & Matthew Holm
Sunny Side Up
Swing It, Sunny
The Babymouse series
The Evil Princess vs. the Brave Knight series
The Squish series
My First Comics series

Also by Jennifer L. Holm
Boston Jane: An Adventure
Boston Jane: Wilderness Days
Boston Jane: The Claim
The Fourteenth Goldfish
The Third Mushroom
Middle School Is Worse Than Meatloaf
Eighth Grade Is Making Me Sick
Our Only May Amelia
The Trouble with May Amelia
Penny from Heaven
Turtle in Paradise
Full of Beans

Also by Matthew Holm
(with Jonathan Follett)
Marvin and the Moths

Random House 🏠 New York

JENNIFER L. HOLM & MATTHEW HOLM

BABYMOUSE
TALES FROM THE LOCKER

School-Tripped

Visit us on the Web! rhcbooks.com

Educators and librarians, for a variety of teaching tools, visit us at RHTeachersLibrarians.com

Library of Congress Cataloging-in-Publication Data
Names: Holm, Jennifer L., author. | Holm, Matthew, author, illustrator.
Title: School-tripped / Jennifer L. Holm and Matthew Holm.
Description: First edition. | New York : Random House, [2019]
Series: Babymouse. Tales from the locker; 3
Summary: "When Babymouse's art class goes on a field trip to the museum, she decides to test her freedom by exploring the big city without a chaperone." —Provided by publisher.
Identifiers: LCCN 2018047500 | ISBN 978-0-399-55444-5 (hardback)
ISBN 978-0-399-55445-2 (glb) | ISBN 978-0-399-55446-9 (epub)
Subjects: | CYAC: School field trips—Fiction. | Adventure and adventurers—Fiction. | Middle schools—Fiction. | Schools—Fiction. | Mice—Fiction. Animals—Fiction. | Humorous stories.
Classification: LCC PZ7.H732226 Sch 2019 | DDC [Fic]—dc23

Printed in the United States of America
10 9 8 7 6 5 4 3 2 1
First Edition

For Myly,
the most adventurous person ever!

Contents

Same Old Middle School

Picture a dark auditorium.

A bright spotlight shines over-head.

A single microphone hums in anticipation.

Slowly pan in on me, Babymouse, sitting on a stool center stage.

I lean forward and begin my monologue.

"I guess I thought middle school would

be exciting. And it was—for maybe three weeks.

"Oh, who am I kidding? Make that one week. The truth was that middle school was just like elementary school, with way more homework, and way fewer arts and crafts projects. It was boring. Nothing exciting ever happened."

SCREECH!

I jumped as I heard a loud noise offstage. A door creaked open, and a janitor appeared, dragging a mop and a rusty bucket of sloshing dirty water. He flipped on the lights to illuminate an empty auditorium.

"Hey!" he barked. "You're not allowed to be here."

I hurried off the stool, embarrassed.

"Sorry," I said quickly. "I had a free period, so I thought I could hang out here."

He sighed and shook his head.

"I'll let it go this time," he said. "But don't let me catch you in here again. . . ."

He didn't have to tell me twice! I gathered my things and hightailed it out of there as fast as I could. So much for freedom of expression!

But anyway, about my take on middle school . . .

It probably sounds like I'm being dramatic. But I'm really not! It had gone from this shiny-new magical experience into another never-ending parade of classes, homework, and popularity contests. (None of which I was winning.)

Here was my life in a nutshell:

☑ 1. Stupid locker?

☑ 2. Gross bathroom?

☑ 3. Smelly gym clothes?

☑ 4. Too much homework?

☑ 5. Messy whiskers?

If only I could click my heels together and disappear into a far-off land of adventure.

Instead, I wandered into the school lobby to check out the "New and Cool!" bulletin board. The sad thing was, not a single thing on the board was new or cool in the slightest.

Seriously, it was the same yellowed flyers as always, probably posted a hundred years ago, when the school was first founded.

(I'm pretty sure some of them were typed on a typewriter!)

NEW AND COOL!

Excited about the

SPACE RACE?

Join the
Space Club
now!

STAMP CLUB!

We know you'll
give it your

"STAMP"

of approval!

The bell rang, and the hallways flooded with students changing classes.

I had gym next period. Which meant I had to play soccer. It wasn't my favorite. Everyone played like sharks.

Plus, unless one of my friends was a team captain, I **always** got picked last. Last time Felicia and Berry were captains, they picked every single possible person except me. You think I'm kidding?

Don't get me wrong. I tried my best, but . . . my best was not very good. (Though I was still better than a rabid squirrel! I think. . . .)

On my way to the locker room, I ran into my best friend, Wilson, in the hallway.

"Hey, Babymouse, heading to gym?" he asked.

"You know it," I replied.

In no time, we had all suited up and taken the field, practicing our shots on goal. (Which meant we didn't need to pick teams—thank goodness!)

When my turn came, I took a running start and kicked the ball with all my might. I ended up missing completely and flew onto my tail at the most slippery part of the field. That would have been bad enough. But instead of just landing and staying put, I **slid** all the way down the field and straight off the side.

Luckily, an enormous mud puddle broke my fall.

I heard a burst of cackling. I covered myself, thinking it was a flock of geese coming to poop on my head. But it was worse. The cackling noise was the popular girls laughing at me from the sidelines.

Story of my life. If I'm not being pooped on by geese, I'm being laughed at by the popular kids.

At least Wilson came over and helped me up.

"It could've been worse, Babymouse," he said.

"How?"

"At least your elbow didn't get muddy."

Le muddy sigh.

My gym teacher came over to check on me. Once she was convinced I didn't have any broken bones, she let me hit the locker room early.

I plodded off the field slowly, **squish, squish, squish**-ing with every step.

Finally, I made it into the school and back down to the girls' locker room. The warm smell of sweat and feet (or maybe it was sweaty feet?) hit me like a ton of bricks, as usual.

I tracked mud all the way to my locker and swiveled the lock until I got the combination right.

Now, if you thought my regular locker was bad—boy, wait till you see my **gym** locker.

Penny and I shared a locker. Let's just say it was obvious whose part was whose.

I was pretty sure I had a clean shirt in the back somewhere, behind my other stuff. The problem was that an old water bottle was lodged in front of it, jammed in the locker. I tugged on it.

Mouse-terpiece

The next day wasn't much of an improvement.

Until I got to art class.

Art was my favorite subject. Mostly because it was the one place where I could let my imagination run a little wild. History was not very creative, and don't get me started on algebra.

We were doing a unit on great artists throughout the centuries. My teacher,

Ms. Painter (yes, that is really her name!), was clicking through slides of some of the world's most famous masterpieces.

I thought it would be a lot of fun to be an artist. I loved painting.

And I had plenty of friends who would be great models.

I wondered if famous artists had to deal with all the same middle-school problems I did.

Did Salvador Dalí have to share a locker?

Did Mary Cassatt ever forget her homework?

Did Vincent van Gogh struggle to learn fractions?

ARTIST'S DAY PLANNER

25 *Wednesday*

8:00	Wake up and think about what to paint.
9:00	Eat croissants.
10:30	Think about what to paint.
11:30	Drink latte at Eiffel Tower.
12:00	Think some more about painting.
1:00	Leisurely lunch.
2:00	Think about what to paint.
3:00	SNACK TIME: chocolate gateaux.
4:00–4:15	Paint.
4:15	Late-afternoon tea.

26

8:00
9:00
10:30
11:30
12:00
1:00
2:00
3:00
4:0
4:

Or did they just get to sit around and be creative?

It seemed like a pretty sweet life, especially the whole eating part. (Who doesn't like chocolate gateaux?)

My sweet dreams of cake disappeared when Ms. Painter clicked on the lights.

She walked to the front of the room. Students lifted their heads off their desks and wiped away the drool. (Except one. My friend Georgie had fallen asleep. I nudged him, and he quickly shot up in his chair— which was pretty obvious, considering he was a giraffe!)

"Class, I have an exciting announcement to make . . . ," Ms. Painter said.

Now, like every other kid, I had learned a long time ago that when a teacher makes an "exciting announcement," it's usually just about the **least** exciting thing in the whole entire world.

But Ms. Painter wasn't one of **those** teachers, so I was actually curious.

"Next week, our class will be going on a special trip," she declared.

A special trip?? I was ecstatic! I loved class trips! (Almost as much as I loved exclamation points!!!!!!!!!!!!!!)

But where could we be going? It had to be somewhere art-related, right? My mind immediately began to scan through all the most artistic cities I could think of. . . .

Paris? **Mais oui!**

London? **Cheerio, old chap!**

Rome? **Grazie! Prego!** Okay, that just means "Thank you" and "You're welcome." I didn't know much Italian. But that was exactly why it would be the perfect place to visit!

Or maybe we would go . . . **somewhere over the rainbow!**

My teacher cleared her throat and continued.

"Anyway, as I was saying, we will be
going on a special trip . . . to the art museum
in the city!"

I looked at Penny, who was sitting next to me. She gave me a huge high five. She loved art just as much as I did.

"That's not all," Ms. Painter went on. "As middle schoolers, we are focusing on the importance of responsibility and independence. Therefore, you will not have chaperones in the museum with you. Instead, we'd like you to stay together in pairs. We will be counting on you to behave respectfully."

No chaperones?

No one to ask for permission to drink from the water fountain.

No one to keep track of us when we used the bathroom.

No one to make us count off by numbers in the parking lot.

It was incredible. It was unbelievable. It was . . .

FREEDOM!

"Any questions?" Ms. Painter asked.

I raised a hand and waved wildly. "Ms. Painter! Ms. Painter!"

"Yes, Babymouse?" Ms. Painter said with a smile. She was the one teacher who appreciated my high level of enthusiasm.

REPORT CARD

ACADEMIC TERM: 2nd

STUDENT: Babymouse

SUBJECT	GRADE	TEACHER'S NOTES
SOCIAL STUDIES	B	Student can be a bit too enthusiastic.
SCIENCE	B+	Enthusiasm sometimes detrac from concentration.
ENGLISH LANG. ARTS	A	Contagious enthusiasm; requ frequent trips to nurse's offic
PHYS. ED.	C	Enthusiasm doesn't translat well into skill building.
ART	A	Fabulous enthusiasm!

"What should we wear? What should we bring?" I asked.

I was all about planning.

"Both good questions, Babymouse," she said. "You can wear whatever you like, so long as you pair it with comfortable shoes. Also, please bring a bag lunch or money. There are food trucks outside the museum."

Upon hearing "food trucks," Wilson almost fell off his chair. "All right!" he mouthed to me.

The bell rang.

"Please take a permission slip with you on the way out," Ms. Painter called over the noise of chairs and desks shifting. "I'll need them signed and returned by Friday in order for you to participate."

I hurried to the front of the room and grabbed a permission slip off her desk.

I knew it was kind of silly, but I was so

excited about the trip that even the **permission slip** seemed exciting to me. Until I actually read it.

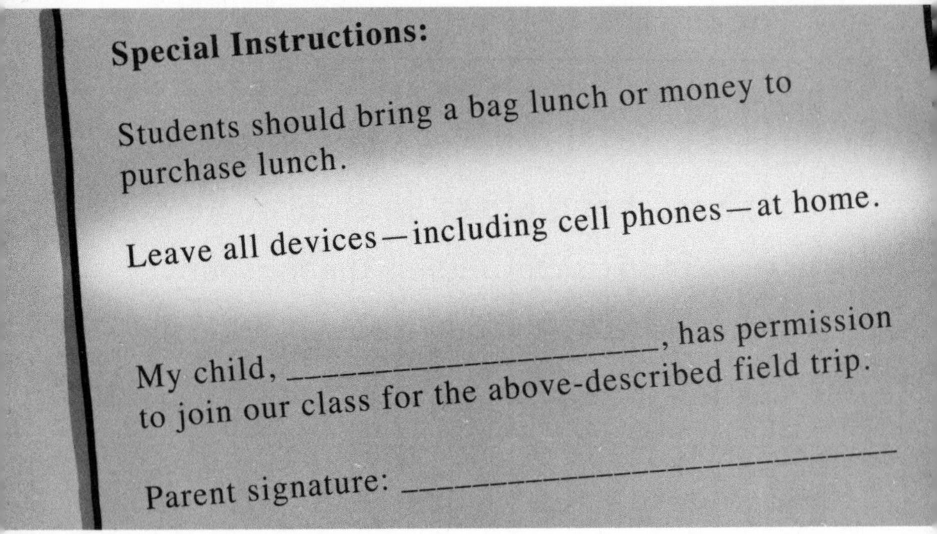

Special Instructions:

Students should bring a bag lunch or money to purchase lunch.

Leave all devices—including cell phones—at home.

My child, _____, has permission to join our class for the above-described field trip.

Parent signature: _____

My face fell. Ever since I'd gotten my Whiz Bang™ phone, I'd taken it everywhere I went. I couldn't just abandon it after everything we'd been through!

Still, I tried to focus on the positive: **I was going on a special class trip into the city!** A special class trip into the city with **no chaperones.** It was thrilling! Finally, I felt I was being treated like a grown-up.

GROWN-UP
CAN DRIVE!
STAY UP ALL NIGHT!
NO HOMEWORK!
PLAY ON DEVICES ALL THE TIME!
EAT WHATEVER YOU WANT, INCLUDING CHOCOLATE GATEAUX!

I practically floated all the way to Locker. It took me several tries to open it, but even that couldn't get me down today. I was so zoned out that I didn't notice Penny coming up behind me.

"Hey, Babymouse!" she said.

"Hey back!"

Penny pointed to the picture I had taped in my locker next to my drawings. "I love Tommy H!"

He was **the** hottest star on Broadway.

TOMMY H, STAR OF KOALATON!

FROM EXECUTIVE PRODUCER FELICIA FURRYPAWS

"So do you want to be class trip buddies?" she asked.

"Definitely!" I exclaimed.

"Cool!" she said. "By the way, that's a really good drawing. You're talented, Babymouse."

She walked away.

I stared at my drawing. Was she right? Was I talented?

Huh. I guess it couldn't hurt to bring some of my OWN artwork on the field trip, just in case the museum curator was looking for an up-and-coming artist to showcase!

RING!

That was the last bell of the day. I got my stuff and sprinted toward the door so I could get a good seat on the bus.

I flew by my gym teacher, who blew her whistle and called after me, "Hey, Babymouse! No running in the halls! Why don't you show that hustle on the soccer field?"

When I reached the bus, I was the first one in line. Huzzah!

The driver pulled the lever to open the door, and I hopped on, looking around. I had the whole bus to myself. It wasn't really about getting the best seat. It was about getting the "least worst" seat.

The back of the bus? **Too bumpy.**

By the wheels? **No legroom.**

Behind the driver? **Nah!**

Maybe in the middle on the left? **The seat was cracked.**

Or on the right? **Yuck! There was bubble gum everywhere.**

The one behind it? **I was not going anywhere near whatever that was on the floor.**

Suddenly, the bus driver yelled, "JUST SIT DOWN, KID!"

I looked up and saw students piled up behind me. I sat in the closest seat.

Right on the gross bubble gum.

Ewwwwwwww.

☆ ♥ ☆

When I got home, I ran inside with the permission slip already in hand.

"Mom!" I yelled, opening every door. "Mom! I need you! It's an emergency!"

Moments later, my mom ran into the kitchen in a bath towel. Soapsuds dripped off her arms and legs and all over the floor.

"I'm here! I'm here!" she yelled. "What's wrong?"

"Mom, I need you to sign my permission slip!"

I thrust the paper in her direction.

"You need me to . . . what now?" she asked, frowning.

I smiled sheepishly and waved the sheet at her.

"We're going on a class trip to the art museum in the city! And there are no chaperones because we're learning independence and responsibility!"

My mom sighed heavily. The permission slip in my hand began to feel like a flag of surrender. Sopping wet, she took it from me and placed it on the table.

"Babymouse," she said seriously. "I think we need to talk about what IS and what is NOT an emergency again."

"Okay," I said slowly. "I'll talk to you after your shower."

She nodded and went back upstairs. "And wipe the floor, please," she called back.

☆ ♥ ☆

Wiping the floor, it turned out, was just one of the many, many things I would have to do to convince my parents I was "independent" and "responsible" enough to join my classmates on an unchaperoned trip to the city.

I had to make my bed every morning, empty and load the dishwasher, help fold the laundry, collect random coffee cups from my mother's office, hang up wet towels in the bathroom, make sure that dirty shoes were left outside, and vacuum our den. I don't know why doing any of these things made me more responsible, but the house sure started to look a whole lot cleaner.

But after a few days of being extra **extra** responsible, and no false-alarm emergencies, I convinced my mom to sign my waterlogged permission slip. I had helpfully filled in the washed-away words.

Special Instructions:

Students should bring a bag lunch or money to purchase lunch.

Leave all devices—*Ex*cluding cell phones—at home.

My child, _Babymouse_, has permission to join our class for the above-described field trip.

Parent signature:

~~Emerald~~ Big City, here I come!

A Work of Art

In the days leading up to the class trip, I worked hard on my art collection whenever I got the chance. I used watercolors, colored pencils, charcoals, and mixed media (a collage kind of thing) until I had a fabulous portfolio I really loved. Surely, the museum curators would see I was a budding talent, ready to bloom into a master artist!

The night before the class trip, everything was finally ready.

That is, everything except I still needed to think of a way to carry my portfolio.

This was easier said than done.

I first looked around the house for something box-shaped, but nothing was quite the right fit.

Shirt boxes were too small.

Board game boxes were too narrow.

Cereal boxes were too . . . crumby.

Still, I couldn't see carrying a hanger around all day, although it was a clever idea.

WE ♥ OUR CUSTOMERS

Defeated, I lay on my bed and stared at the wall. The perfect smile of Tommy H smiled back at me from my new poster.

I still had the cardboard tube it had come in. Maybe I could use that to store my art?

It turned out to be a great solution. Everything fit perfectly, and this way my art wouldn't get crumpled.

I was really proud of myself. I had worked hard on my art collection, and no matter what happened, that made me feel like a "real" artist.

"Way to go, Babymouse!" I proudly said to my mirror.

I quickly washed up, put on my pj's, and climbed under the covers.

The next morning, I jumped out of bed even before my phone alarm went off. It was the big day! Finally!

Then I realized I had been so busy worrying about my artwork that I hadn't thought about what to wear! I whipped open my closet and started tossing clothes onto my bed.

Someone knocked on the door.

"Who is it?" I called.

"Me," said my little brother, Squeak. "Can I come in?"

"Sure."

"What are you doing?" he asked, looking around.

"I'm trying to find a cool outfit to wear to the city!"

"A **cool** outfit?" he said with a smile. "I know what you should wear."

"Yeah?" I asked skeptically. I usually didn't trust him on matters of fashion, but it was cute that he wanted to help his big sister.

Squeak returned a minute later ... with my snowsuit.

I waved him out of my room and looked at the clock. I had to make a decision soon if I wanted to be on time—and not get stuck with the gum seat again!

(STUCK, ha. But no time for jokes!)

I looked at my options.

Finally, I decided on a classic white shirt, a denim skirt, and a bright-red pair of patent-leather high-heel pumps. Ms. Painter had said to wear comfortable shoes, but we were going to the city! And nobody wants to get discovered wearing stinky old tennis shoes. (Except maybe a tennis player. But you know what I mean.)

I didn't want to drag around my backpack all day, so I grabbed a basket-style purse from my closet instead. Perfect!

"Babymouse, you're going to be late!" Dad called from downstairs.

"Coming!" I yelled back.

I grabbed my Whiz Bang™ and stared at it, feeling a little (just a little) guilty. I knew the permission slip said we couldn't bring our cell phones on the trip—but the Whiz Bang™ wasn't just **any** cell phone. It was my connection to the world and everyone in it!

Besides, it was good in an emergency. Like if I got separated from Penny. Or they ran out of chocolate gateaux at the museum snack bar. This way, I could just call for takeout. (Cakeout?)

That settled it. I was taking my Whiz Bang™ along, and there was nothing anyone could do to stop me. With that, I tossed the Whiz Bang™ into my basket and grabbed my tube of art. I was ready to go.

Mom and Squeak were sitting at the

table eating breakfast. Dad was at the stove making pancakes.

"Got to go!" I announced, grabbing a granola bar. "See you later!"

"Wait a second, Babymouse," Mom said. "Aren't you forgetting something?"

Could she have found out about the phone? Was I totally busted?

"What do you mean?" I asked, shifting uneasily from foot to foot.

She gave me a funny look.

"Your lunch!" Dad said, tossing me a brown paper bag from across the room.

I laughed nervously as I caught it. "Oh, right. Thanks, guys!"

"Have a great day!" Mom called after me.

Glamour-A-Go-Go!

I made it to the bus stop just as the bus was pulling up. I was practically bouncing with excitement. I climbed on and looked around for my friends. Penny waved to me from the back. She had saved a seat for me. "Thanks," I said, sliding in next to her.

"Big day!" she said.

"Yep, finally!" I replied.

"How do you think we're going to be

traveling to the city?" she asked me.

"Hmm . . . ," I replied. "I hadn't thought of that."

Suddenly, my mind was alive with possibilities.

I immediately pictured a stretch limousine big enough to fit my entire class. We would pop bottles of lemonade, sing karaoke, and dance under a sparkly disco ball all the way to the museum. We'd watch our small town slowly fade away, replaced by the bright lights of the big city.

"Maybe we'll take a limousine!" I exclaimed.

Felicia scoffed at me from across the aisle. "Sounds like someone's been staring into bright lights too long," she yawned.

I turned red.

"Okay, well, if not a limousine, then maybe a super-luxury RV!"

I pictured an oversize RV packed with a fully stocked fridge, a milk shake machine, Ping-Pong tables, a wide-screen TV, and reclining movie-theater seats. We could call it the Glamour-A-Go-Go!

"Keep dreaming, Babymouse," Felicia said.

☆ ♥ ☆

We met in the art room so Ms. Painter could take attendance. Not surprisingly, everyone was present.

"Great!" Ms. Painter said, checking the last name off her list. "The school bus will be here any minute."

My heart sank. Another school bus? Seriously? I looked way too chic to arrive at the museum on a boring old school bus.

Le sigh.

We filed out of the room and toward the front lobby.

"Remember," Ms. Painter said. "Everyone needs to stay with their partner . . . or in this case, your 'art-ner.'"

Penny and I stayed together. Wilson and Georgie did, too. They had paired up for the day.

I stepped onto the bus and was hit with a strong whiff of something awful.

"Ew!" yelled my friend Duckie from the back of the bus, holding up a moldy green plastic bag. "Someone left a tuna sandwich here!" From the smell, I was guessing they'd left it there **last** school year.

Everyone groaned as our teacher instructed us to open the windows.

Maybe this was why Leonardo da Vinci tried to invent a flying machine—to avoid stinky buses!

After yesterday's gum fiasco, I decided it would be best to let Penny choose our seats. We climbed into a two-seater behind Felicia and her friends, who were whispering excitedly.

I couldn't help but (purposely) overhear snippets of their conversation.

"So everyone is still good with the plan?" Felicia asked.

Melinda, Belinda, and Berry whispered, "Yes."

"As soon as possible, we ditch the art museum and head into the city. We start at Kazoo. That's the clothing boutique I texted you guys about, where all the celebs are shopping these days. Then we grab lunch at Epic, the famous sushi place downtown. Later, we go to the Theater District to see if we can snag tickets to **Koalaton,** starring—"

"Tommy H!" they all squealed in unison.

I couldn't believe it! Felicia and her friends were sneaking off by themselves for a whole day of city fun? No fair!

But mostly I was jealous of them seeing **Koalaton** with Tommy H.

I immediately began to rethink my day at the art museum. I knew I had agreed to the terms of the trip, and that the whole point of us having no chaperones was to prove we didn't need them—but this was a once-in-a-lifetime opportunity to see Tommy H!

Soon after, we pulled up to the art museum. I grabbed my basket and poster tube as we rushed off the bus.

Ms. Painter herded us into the lobby of the museum. It was covered in glistening marble, with lots of cool tall columns.

In the center of the floor was a bright-yellow sun made out of brick-like mosaic tiles. It was like my very own yellow brick road! Who knew where it would lead?!

"Now, students," Ms. Painter said. "Do check out as many exhibits as possible, but be sure to meet back here by five o'clock at the latest."

"MOST IMPORTANTLY," she continued,

"do not wander away from the museum. You may only go outside to get lunch at the food trucks, and then immediately come back inside. Am I understood?"

The class gave a loud "Yes, Ms. Painter," after which she released us to go exploring.

Most of my classmates immediately poured into the museum. But before I rushed off with the masses, I had business to attend to.

"Hold on a sec, Penny," I told her. "I have to do something really fast."

"No problem," Penny replied. "I'm going to check out the museum map over there."

I approached the information desk. There was an older lady sitting behind it.

"Excuse me," I said.

"Hello. May I help you?" she asked.

"Are you the museum curator?"

She smiled warmly. "No, I'm a volunteer. Is there something I can help you with?"

"I wanted to show my art collection to the museum curator, please."

"I see," she said. "That's great that you're an artist! But unfortunately, the museum doesn't accept unsolicited portfolios."

My heart sank. I didn't know what "unsolicited" meant, but I was pretty sure she was politely saying no.

"But I'll tell you what," she continued. "We do have young artists' programs from time to time, so you can follow us online and maybe get involved that way."

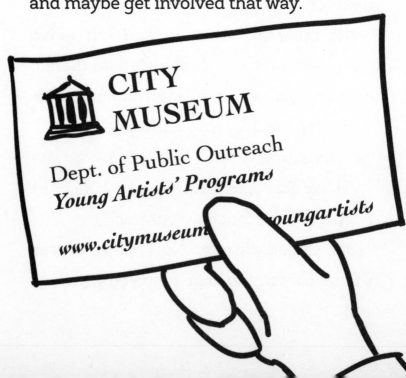

CITY
MUSEUM

Dept. of Public Outreach
Young Artists' Programs

www.citymuseum   oungartists

"Thanks!" I said. "Do you think I could leave my art with you anyway, so I don't have to carry it around the museum all day?"

"My shift is almost over. But we actually have a coat-and-item check right across the way," she said, pointing. "So you can store your things safely there."

I looked to where she was pointing, but instead of seeing the coat check, my eyes lit upon the gift shop right next to it.

"Okay, great!" I waved good-bye and went to track down Penny.

We stopped briefly at the coat check, where a man handed me a number slip and a hanger. This made me laugh, because if I had just gone with the hanger idea, I would be all set right now!

Instead, he stored my poster tube in a cubby in the back.

I took a deep breath as we walked into

the glowing museum shop next door. The shop was full of all sorts of incredible stuff: key chains, scarves, umbrellas, tote bags, books, posters, pencils, and everything in between.

"Hey! There's Wilson and Georgie!" Penny called, waving.

They were checking out the postcards. There were hundreds of them, and each one was more beautiful than the last. (To be honest, I didn't really get the whole point of mailing a postcard. From what I'd heard, it was some medieval form of communication, from back before there was reliable Wi-Fi.)

"How do I look?" Penny asked, donning a tote bag and dramatically throwing a scarf over her shoulder. She was so good at that.

"Fantastique, mon amie!" I said with a smile.

It was then that I saw the most magical thing I had ever seen: a silver spoon with a little painting on it!

"Wilson, can you believe your eyes?" I asked in disbelief.

Wilson rubbed his eyes, confused. "It just looks like a fancy spoon to me."

"No, no, no," I responded. "You're missing the whole point!"

"If anything, the spoon is missing a point. Get it? Like a fork or a knife?" he asked.

Georgie slapped Wilson on the back. "Good one," he said, laughing.

"There is a painting **on the spoon**!" I said.

Wilson furrowed his brow. "Uh, you know they have the **real** paintings hanging in the museum, right, Babymouse?"

"I **need** that spoon, Wilson!" I exclaimed, ignoring him.

A cranky-looking salesman came over.

"Would you like to **buy** something?" he asked me.

I swallowed hard. "How much does this spoon cost?"

The salesman gave me a disapproving look. "This is a limited-edition collector's spoon," he replied.

I held it up to catch the light.

In the glint of the spoon, I saw something over my shoulder. I spun around to see Felicia and her friends sneaking out of the lobby bathroom and toward the exit.

"They're leaving!" I called to Penny.

The salesman looked confused.

"I'm sorry," I said, and handed him the spoon. "I have to go now. Thanks for your help."

He harrumphed as he placed the spoon back in its case. I ran out.

Penny, Georgie, and Wilson dropped what they were doing and ran after me.

"Where are you going?" Georgie asked.

"Felicia and her friends are sneaking out of the museum to spend the day in the city," I told him.

"Sounds like trouble to me," said Wilson.

"What about you, Penny?" I asked. "Do you want to follow them?"

Penny bit her lip. I could tell she was torn.

"It's up to you," I said nonchalantly. "But remember, **every day is an adventure**," I continued, breaking into the **Koalaton** theme song.

"Ugh," Wilson and Georgie groaned, covering their ears.

Penny's face lit up. "Ev-ery day. Ev-ery day. If only you le-e-et it beee," she sang back, giving me a high five. "Let's do it!"

"See you guys later!" I said.

I waved good-bye to Wilson and Georgie as I hurried out a small side door labeled "Not an Exit."

"Babymouse, wait!" Penny shouted.

Such was the beginning of our fabulous
city adventure.

Wrong Turn

Though my shortcut was a bit of a disaster, it did save us time in the end. I climbed over the boxes, and in minutes Penny and I were on the street, just steps behind Felicia and her friends.

I really wanted to hop in a cab and yell "Follow those girls!" but I didn't want to waste precious spoon money. Plus, from the looks of it, the cabs were going more slowly than we could travel on foot.

We followed them through a maze of streets. It wasn't easy, because we had to stay close enough to watch where they were going, but far enough away that they couldn't see us following them. I felt like I was in a spy movie.

The city was incredible. Everywhere I turned, there was something new to see: towering buildings, fancy stores and restaurants, and vendor carts on the street selling soft pretzels and hot dogs. I wondered if any of them sold chocolate gateaux.

Finally, we ended up in a huge outdoor square.

I was trying to decide whether to follow them around all day, or ask them to let us go with them. But in the end, it didn't matter, because a huge bus went by and we lost sight of them completely. Felicia and company had disappeared.

We were on our own.

"Babymouse!" Penny cried, realizing. "They're gone! We're lost!"

"Don't panic, Penny," I said, taking a deep breath. "I'm sure we'll figure something out."

At that moment, a giant costumed monster came toward us.

"You look like you could use a hug," he said in a muffled voice.

Penny wasn't so sure, but I saw lots of small children hugging other characters and having their pictures taken, so I thought, **Why not?**

I gave the monster a big hug as Penny took a photo on my Whiz Bang™. The monster's fur smelled kind of like the school bus, but the hug did make me feel a little bit better.

I pulled away, and the monster put out his hand. I gave it a high five.

"I don't want a high five," the monster said. "I want a tip!"

"Oh," I said, looking down at my chafing shoes. "Here's a tip: don't wear heels if you plan to walk all over the city!"

The monster was not amused. "A **money** tip," he said.

Penny and I looked at each other. A tip just for a hug and a picture? Maybe I should rethink my art career.

I handed the monster a dollar. He pretended to cry when he saw how little it was, but finally he left to go rip off some other kid.

"Man!" I said. "What a weird place."

Penny nodded. "Yeah, and why would . . ." She broke off. "Look! A cat!"

"No more characters, please!" I wailed.

"No, a real cat!" she said. "Actually, I think it's a kitten. Over there!"

I looked where she was pointing, and saw a tiny gray kitten hiding in an alleyway nearby.

We crossed the street and went into the alley.

"There she is!" Penny said.

The gray kitten was sitting in an old pizza box, chewing on stale crusts.

"Here, kitty, kitty," I said gently, putting my hand out.

The kitten took a curious step toward us.

"She's not running away!" Penny whispered excitedly.

"Probably because we still smell like tuna from the bus this morning," I replied.

"Aw, she's so cute!" Penny gushed. "Look at how little she is. She needs our help!"

I nodded. "And a name. Let's call her Pizza Kitty!"

"Agreed!" Penny said. "What should we do with her?"

I cleared a space in my basket and made a soft bed out of a packet of tissues.

"Perfect!" Penny said.

"Purr-fect!" I corrected her.

We put my basket on the ground and gently encouraged the kitten to go inside.

She was shy at first, but once she felt how soft the tissue bed was, she snuggled right in.

"Aw, good little Pizza Kitty," Penny said. "Have you lost your mommy?"

"Or your mittens?" I asked.

Pizza Kitty just closed her eyes and began to fall asleep.

I carefully picked up my basket, and Penny and I got to work searching for the kitten's mother. We looked for a long time, but there were no other cats to be found.

Finally, I saw something.

"Check it out!" I called to Penny, pointing at a flyer taped on a pole of a street sign.

"That looks just like Pizza Kitty!" I exclaimed.

"It IS her," Penny agreed. "We have to bring her back home!"

I took the flyer off the pole and entered the address on my Whiz Bang™, but there was no 1026 Pea Street in the whole city.

"How can that be?" Penny asked, puzzled.

I looked more closely at the flyer. The writing was all running together, kind of like on my permission slip.

"I think this is only part of the address," I told Penny. "It looks like it got soaked in the rain."

Penny nodded.

"Yeah, I think you're right," she said. "We'll have to find her owner another way."

"I know!" I said. "We can look up street names that start with 'Pea' on my Whiz Bang™!"

"Yes! Great idea!" Penny said.

I felt a little guilty about bringing my phone, but at least now I was using it for a good cause. We were kitten rescuers!

I started scrolling, but stopped when I heard Penny gasp.

"Look! A mime!" she said. She pointed across the street to where a young man in black-and-white clothes was standing on the corner.

"And he's miming hailing a cab!" I said. "That's pretty impressive."

A cab pulled over, and he got in.

"Oh," I said. "Guess he wasn't miming after all."

Just then, loud music began blaring, and a crowd of twenty or so people ran past us, all doing a synchronized dance. A teenage girl bumped into me, and my Whiz Bang™

went flying. It hit the ground with a **SMASH** and got kicked to the curb by another dancer rushing past.

Stunned, we watched the dance crew go by in a wave of motion and song. Finally, there was a crescendo of noise and a big finish. The music stopped, and everyone quickly dispersed. A minute later, it was as if nothing had ever happened at all.

"What is going on?" I asked Penny.

"It's a flash mob," Penny explained. "A group of dancers that does surprise performances. I've watched a bunch of videos online."

I walked over to the gutter, where my broken phone lay in a puddle of garbage and sewer water. The shattered screen blinked once, then turned off for good.

"More like a SMASH mob," I groaned. My parents would not be happy. I could already see a lot of chores in my future.

Pounding the Pavement

Now we're lost, with a lost kitten, and we don't even have a cell phone!" Penny exclaimed.

"What about your cell phone?" I asked.

"Some of us actually follow the rules, Babymouse," she said.

"What are we going to do?"

Penny looked across the street. "Hey, isn't that a pay phone?"

"Before there were cell phones," Penny explained, "people had to use pay phones. There's a slot where you put in coins. My grandma told me about them."

At the pay phone, we found a gross old phone book (another thing I'd never seen before) with an alphabetical list of the streets in the city. Penny tore out the page that started with "Pea."

Paxton Pla...

Peach Street

Peacock Street

Peanut Street

Pearl Street

...ble Terrace

We decided to head to Peach Street first. But we still didn't have a phone or a map, so we had to flag down a passing cyclist for directions.

"Excuse me," I said politely. "Can you please point me in the direction of Peach Street?"

"Sure," he replied. "Make a left at the next street, then walk twenty blocks north. That will get you pretty close."

TWENTY blocks? My hopes sank. My feet were **really** starting to hurt. Talk about suffering for fashion.

"Thanks," I said, disheartened.

"Anytime. Cute kitten, by the way!" With that, he rode off.

We followed the bike guy's directions. But soon, my feet had gone from bad to worse. I suddenly wished I had worn my stinky old tennis shoes. My eyes started to tear up.

"What's wrong?" Penny asked.

"My feet are KILLING me!" I replied, showing her the massive blisters on my poor ankles.

"Ouch!" Penny said. "I think we need to take a detour to find you some new shoes. Let's try that boutique down the block."

We walked (I hobbled) down to the boutique, which was worth it. Because the window was filled with all sorts of adorable shoes.

"This place looks great!" I said.

But the minute we stepped (hobbled) through the door, the saleslady shook her head.

"Sorry, girls," she said. "No pets allowed in the boutique!"

"So unfair," I told Penny as we walked out the door.

"Seriously!" she agreed.

The next place we tried was a party-supply store. I didn't want to bother, but Penny insisted.

"You never know when you might get lucky!" she said excitedly, trying on a sparkly tiara. Luck hadn't been on my side, but what did I have to lose?

"Excuse me, do you happen to sell shoes?" I asked the teenage employee.

"Sure. Aisle ten," he said, pointing to the back of the store.

(Note to self: it's never a good sign when an employee directs you to the back of the store.)

When I got to aisle ten, I immediately regretted letting Penny talk me into trying this place.

We headed out (without the shoes, thank you very much!) and walked until we got to a corner pharmacy.

"I'm going to get some bandages to cover my blisters," I told Penny.

"Good call," she said. "We can also pick up some water and kitten food."

Pizza Kitty meowed affectionately, almost as if she understood.

On my way to the first-aid aisle, I passed a rack of cheap plastic flip-flops.

"Bingo!" I yelled.

Penny peeked her head around the corner. "What? You decided you want the clown shoes?"

"No! I found flip-flops!"

I found my size and tried them on. They were a bit flimsy and bright orange, but at this point, I couldn't afford to be fashionable. I needed something comfortable, and these fit the bill!

We headed to the registers in the front of the store.

While Penny was paying, I noticed a disposable-camera display.

"Hey! Maybe we should get a disposable camera," I told her. "We can document little kitty in the big city!"

"Great idea!" Penny said, giving me a thumbs-up.

I added one to my shopping basket.

"What a cute kitten!" the sales associate said as she rang up my things. "Okay, that will be $15.32."

"Wow!" I said. "That's more than I expected."

"Do you want the adorable-pet discount?" she asked with a smile.

"Is that a real thing?!" I asked.

"No," she replied. "I was just joking."

"Oh."

I forked over a twenty-dollar bill and waited for my change. I would have to be really careful if I didn't want to run out of cash.

Within minutes, we were sitting on a bench outside the store with supplies in hand. I patched up my feet while Penny pried open a small can of cat food and poured a cup of water.

"Thanks, I'm super thirsty!" I said, guzzling it down.

"Babymouse! That's for Pizza Kitty!" Penny laughed, filling another cup.

We both laughed. It had been a long morning, and we hadn't even hit the first address yet.

I looked at my watch. It was almost eleven a.m.

"We better hurry if we don't want to get lost in the city forever!" I warned.

"Hey, look!" Penny said. "There's a subway entrance! We should be able to find a map of the city there."

"Good plan," I agreed. "Let's get a photo before we go."

I slipped the camera out of its packaging and snapped a quick picture of the three of us on the bench.

Then we gathered our things and headed down into the subway.

The search had begun!

Subway Series

In the subway station, we found a map of the city, but unfortunately, it only listed the streets on the train routes. We couldn't find Peach Street anywhere.

I stared at the map until my eyes zoned out. The routes were outlined in different bright colors that zigzagged crazily across the city. Oddly enough, it reminded me of a modern painting of squiggly lines.

City Subway System Map

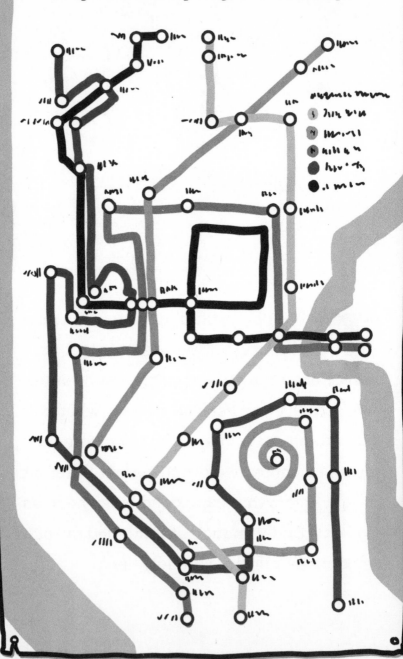

"Have you ever taken the subway before?" Penny asked.

I shook my head. "How hard can it be?"

We bought subway cards and swiped them at the entryway. Then we went down a bunch of steps and onto a platform. There were train tracks on both sides.

"Which way should we go?" Penny asked.

I looked for a long time down the dark, empty tunnel. No clues there. Then I looked at the people waiting, to see which side looked more like cat people.

"Let's just get on whichever one comes first," Penny suggested.

"Sounds good to me," I said, sitting on a bench. I was tired from all the walking.

Just then, a train came.

"Let's go, Babymouse," she said.

As I stood up, I felt something sticky. I looked at the bench.

"Babymouse!" Penny shouted.

I sprinted toward the train. (My soccer coach would have been proud.)

"Stand clear of the closing doors, please," a voice boomed over a loudspeaker.

But before I was all the way in, the doors shut, catching the back of my shirt. This was worse than my stupid locker!

Finally, I tugged my shirt and was free.

Penny and I were able to find seats together near a window. I looked through the glass and saw something surprising—the mime we had seen earlier was on a train passing in the opposite direction!

"Look," Penny whispered, pointing.

"The mime? I know! I saw him, too," I replied. "He sure gets around!"

Penny shook her head and pointed toward a sign on the wall.

ABSOLUTELY NO PETS

"Uh-oh." I swallowed hard.

Pizza Kitty, who had been pretty quiet all day, immediately began to purr. Typical.

We stayed on the train for a long time.

"When should we get off? Penny asked.

Suddenly, the brakes lurched to a grind-ing halt.

"Last stop on the train," the loudspeaker bellowed. "Please exit the train car."

We got off the train and followed the dark platform to the exit. When we finally stepped outside, our eyes blinked in the bright sun. I couldn't believe it! It looked like we were at the beach!

"I don't think we're in the city anymore, Pizza Kitty," I said slowly.

Le lost sigh.

☆ ♡ ☆

After asking about one hundred people—all of whom seemed to tell us to go in opposite directions—we finally made it to one of the streets on our list: Peacock Street.

We arrived at a house that had "1026 Peacock" spray-painted on the garage. I shivered.

Nothing about the place seemed welcoming, or peacock-like.

"Are you sure we should be doing this?" Penny asked nervously.

"Not really," I answered honestly, "but we've come too far to turn back now."

Literally.

We cautiously walked through a gate in a chain-link fence, then up to the front door. I knocked and stepped back. Nothing happened.

There was a sign that read "Deliveries" next to a doorbell. I pressed the buzzer.

Loud growling noises came from inside. Pizza Kitty yelped and hid as far down in my basket as she could go.

That's when we turned around and realized the growling noises weren't coming from inside.

They were coming from . . . OUTSIDE.

The whole yard was full of big, scary guard dogs with sharp teeth.

"I think we should go," Penny whispered. "Don't make any sudden movements."

"Got it," I said.

KICK!   CLANK!

As if the sound was a starter pistol, the snarling dogs chased after us, barking and growling angrily. Penny, Pizza Kitty, and I lunged through the gate just in time, shutting it hard behind us.

The dogs snapped at me as I quickly put the latch back.

Penny and I nearly collapsed with relief. Pizza Kitty looked terrified.

After a minute, we finally caught our breath, at which point I saw a huge sign on the gate.

We crossed "Peacock Street" off our list.

Paxton Pl...

Peach Street

~~Peacock Street~~

Peanut Street

Pearl Street

...bble Terrace

The Wizard of Dumplings

The only thing to do was reverse our steps and go back the way we came. We hopped on the subway and headed toward the city.

After about thirty minutes of starting and stopping, my stomach was growling louder than the Peacock Street dogs.

GRRRRUUUMMMBBLE...

"Hungry?" Penny asked.

"Really hungry," I replied. "Let's get off at the next stop to eat."

The next stop was Chinatown. We jumped off (avoiding the closing doors this time!) and exited the station.

Penny and I plopped down onto a street curb. I reached into my bag and realized I had left my lunch on the bus!

"I guess the bus is going to stink on the way home, too," I said with a facepalm.

As it turned out, Penny had planned on buying lunch from the food trucks, so she had extra money. We decided to pool our cash to see how much we had left. I emptied my pockets, and Penny did the same. It didn't look very good.

"What did we even BUY?" I asked.

GUURRRGGLE...

I totaled the leftover money.

"Nine dollars and fourteen cents," I announced.

Right then, a teenage girl walked by and dropped a dollar into Pizza Kitty's basket.

"What a cute kitten!" she said.

Penny and I looked at each other, surprised. Then she shrugged and announced, "Ten dollars and fourteen cents!"

My mind immediately went to Felicia. She, Melinda, Belinda, and Berry were probably in the middle of a glamorous sushi lunch.

Well, no matter. We would just have to find our own fabulous lunch.

Penny had the same idea.

A delicious smell wafted through the air.

"Hey, do you smell that?" I asked.

"Yum! I think it must be from that dumpling place," she said, pointing.

最好餃子
BEST DUMPLINGS!

"Let's check it out!" I said.

The outside of the place looked plain, but the inside was absolutely magical! Near the counter were trays and trays of plump, juicy dumplings!

"Excuse me, how many dumplings can we get for ten dollars and fourteen cents?" I asked the man behind the counter.

Penny dumped all our money out.

The man smiled and said, "I'll see what I can do."

He led us to a cozy table near the front window.

Within minutes, he brought us a pot of tea and steaming baskets of hot golden dumplings. Penny and I marveled at their perfect presentation—they looked almost too good to eat! ("Almost" being the key word—we were starving!)

They were the most delicious dumplings I had ever tasted!

"This guy is the Wizard of Dumplings!" I said.

Penny nodded enthusiastically. Her mouth was too full to say anything.

When the bill came at the end of the meal, it was exactly $10.14, including tax and tip. I couldn't believe it, because we had had sooo much food. (I think he gave us a break just to be nice.)

"What a cute kitten!" he said as we paid the bill. "Wait here a second."

In a moment, he returned with a takeout bag.

"A doggy bag for your furry friend," he said with a smile.

"Thank you so much!" Penny and I said in unison.

"Though maybe in this case, we should call it a kitty bag!" I added.

We all laughed and waved good-bye.

"I'm so stuffed!" I said, back on the street again.

"Me too," Penny replied. "Glad we're going to do more walking!"

We wandered through neighborhood after neighborhood. Soon, we stumbled upon a long line of people that stretched around multiple city blocks. There was no end in sight!

"What do you think they're waiting for?" Penny asked.

"Only one way to find out!" I replied, walking over.

The last person on line was a woman with a baby carriage.

"Excuse me," I said. "What are you all waiting for?"

The woman smiled and showed me a picture on her phone of a funny-looking circular thing.

Pearl Street Pastries "Rolls" Out "Hot" New Bagel

TODAY | 8:48 A.M.

This blogger's favorite bakery is releasing a new inside-out bagel at its **1025 Pearl Street** location today. The bagel is doughy on the outside and crunchy on the inside. Everyone in the city wants to get their hands on it!

"Oooh," I said. "Good luck!"

"Did you see that?" Penny asked as we walked away.

"Yeah," I replied. "Looks delicious!"

"No," she said. "**Pearl Street!** That's one of the streets on our list!"

Aha!

We followed the line from end to beginning as it wound around block after block. These people seriously, **seriously** wanted that inside-out bagel.

Finally, we got to the storefront at 1025 Pearl Street. Sure enough, there were streamers, posters, and sandwich boards all announcing the one-of-a-kind inside-out bagel. I looked closely at the picture.

"I don't get it," I told Penny. "It just looks like a weird bagel to me."

"Over there!" said Penny. "Is that Felicia?"

It was Felicia. And Melinda, Belinda, and

Berry. They were next in line to buy inside-out bagels!

"Let's go catch up with them!" I said, trying to make my way into the store. "Felicia! Hey!"

"HEY! WAIT YOUR TURN!" a woman yelled angrily.

"YEAH!" said another. "We've been here for hours!"

Suddenly, everyone in the line began yelling and booing.

A man in a black suit with a badge that said "Pastry Patrol" was immediately on the scene.

"Ma'am, I'm going to need you to vacate the premises," he said.

"But I just wanted to see—"

"Ma'am, do you want me to call for bakery backup?" he asked, putting his walkie-talkie close to his mouth.

"It's okay," said Penny, pulling me aside. "We were just leaving."

The crowd clapped and cheered as we were escorted away from the store.

"That was embarrassing," I said, collapsing onto an empty stoop.

"Look on the bright side," said Penny. "We can cross another street off our list."

She pointed at "1026 Pearl Street" on a window across the street. The place was an empty storefront. A large "For Rent" sign hung in the window.

"Two down, two to go!" I said enthusiastically.

I pulled a pen from my basket and crossed "Pearl Street" off our list.

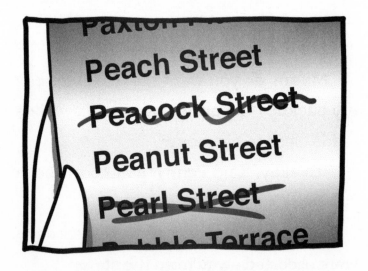

Peanut and Peach? Two tasty streets to go.

Exit Stage Left

I looked at my watch. It was almost two p.m. We still had a lot of ground to cover if we wanted to get Pizza Kitty back to her owner—and make it to the bus before it left the museum!

"Where to now?" Penny asked, holding out our dwindling list of street names.

"Hopefully somewhere with a bathroom!" I replied. I'd drunk a LOT of tea at lunch.

Penny and I looked around. The streets

had become more crowded with people. That's when we saw him AGAIN—the mysterious mime was sitting on a fire escape around the corner!

"The mime!" I exclaimed.

"What are the chances?" Penny asked. "And where are we, anyway?"

I looked up at a street sign.

THE THEATER DISTRICT

Celebrating

100
YEARS

of
Magical
Storytelling

"Looks like we're in—"

"THE Theater District?!" Penny cut me off (with **style**, I might add).

The fire escape was behind a theater! I could almost see Penny's eyes transforming into stars as she took it all in. Theater was one of her all-time favorite things. Don't get me wrong, I like theater just as much as the next mouse—but the bathroom situation was turning into an emergency.

(Cue Mom's "what IS or is NOT an emergency" speech. You know what I mean!)

"Let's go ask the mime if he knows of any public bathrooms," Penny suggested.

Pizza Kitty meowed in agreement. Maybe she had to go, too.

I really wasn't looking forward to translating mime directions, but it seemed about as good as any other option.

We walked slowly toward the fire escape, where we realized the mime was munching on French fries. He stared as we came closer. At first, I thought it was because I was walking funny (reminder: bathroom

situation!), but then I realized he was staring at Pizza Kitty's adorable head poking
out of my basket.

"What a cute kitten!" he said. He emptied
the rest of the French fries into his mouth
and slid off the fire escape.

"We're trying to find her owner," Penny
replied.

"Aw," he said, putting out his gloved
hand. "Can I see her?"

Penny lifted the basket top, and the
mime began nonsensically baby-talking to
the kitten.

WHUT A
CUTE WITTLE
MITTEN KITTEN,
AWWWW. . . .

"I thought mimes didn't talk," I said, confused.

"I'm on my lunch break," he replied. He crumpled up his fast-food bag and tossed it into a nearby trash can.

"Oh, in that case, can we use the theater restroom?" I asked.

"Well, I'm not supposed to let people backstage," he said slowly. "But the security guard loves cats, so he might make an exception."

He led the way toward a back entrance. Outside it, a couple of people were sitting around on old milk crates, playing cards. Some of them waved as we went by. The mime nodded and held open the large metal door.

"Friends of yours, H?" asked the burly security guard inside the door.

I shrank back. I was not looking to get escorted out of **two** places in one day.

"Something like that," he replied with a grin. "Look what they got in the basket."

He pointed to Pizza Kitty, and the security guard's demeanor instantly changed.

"What a cute kitten!" he squealed. Then he said, serious again, "Sure, go on through. Just keep it down because they're still rehearsing for tonight."

The mime flashed a smile.

Something about his smile seemed so familiar to me. . . .

The theater was empty except for a handful of actors rehearsing onstage. I handed Pizza Kitty to Penny and bolted to the nearest bathroom.

When I returned, I found her sitting in the back row with the mime, watching the rehearsal. I took Pizza Kitty so Penny could use the bathroom, then sat and watched the incredible choreography unfold onstage.

A woman with a clipboard and a headset approached. I thought for sure I was going to get kicked out, but instead she motioned past me, toward the mime.

"Tommy, you're next for hair and makeup," she said, tapping her watch. "We're starting at act two."

Before I could understand what was going on, she had disappeared into the back of the theater.

"That's my director," said the mime. "Gotta go!"

I sat in silence, stunned.

"What was that about?" Penny asked, returning from the bathroom.

"Penny," I said slowly. "You're not going to believe this, but you know that, um, mime?"

"Yeah, what a nice guy! For a mime, I mean. That seems like it would be a weird job, you know? Just wandering around all day not talking and—"

I cut her off. "That mime is Tommy H!"

Her mouth dropped open.

Penny and I sat watching the rehearsal, mesmerized. It was the best show we had ever seen—and we weren't even really **seeing** it!

When the rehearsal finally ended, it took everything in our power to pry ourselves away from our seats. But the clock was ticking, and we still had to find Pizza Kitty's home.

☆ ♥ ☆

As luck would have it, we bumped into Tommy H on our way out the side door. (Okay, I admit it: we waited around for almost half an hour. . . .)

"Can we pleeeeease have your autograph?" Penny asked, wasting no time.

"Sure," he said, adjusting the duffel bag over his shoulder. "As long as I can take a picture with your kitten."

"No problem," I said, lifting the basket. "Pizza Kitty loves photo ops."

"Pizza Kitty?" he asked, taking out his phone. "That's a new one."

"It's a long story," Penny said with a laugh.

"Say 'cheese'!" Tommy H said.

"You mean 'extra cheese'?" I asked, snapping another on my disposable.

Tommy H laughed. (I made Tommy H laugh!)

"Wow, what's with **that** camera?" he asked. "That's so last century."

"Another long story," Penny replied.

"Now, what do you want me to sign?" he asked.

It was then I realized I didn't have any paper. Penny and I turned out our pockets once more, frantically trying to find something other than the scrap of paper with the street names.

"No worries," he said coolly. "You can take these instead."

He reached into a pocket of his duffel bag and handed us each one of his white gloves, which we immediately put on our hands.

We thanked him and waved good-bye (with his gloves) just as a black SUV pulled up to the curb. The door opened, and Tommy H got in. And just like that, he was gone.

Penny and I stared at each other in disbelief.

"Did that really just happen?" I asked.

"Yes," said a voice from behind me. I turned around to see the security guard chuckling to himself. I smiled awkwardly, and Penny and I started walking down the street in no particular direction.

"I'm never going to take this glove off again!" She held her gloved hand to her cheek.

"That's funny," I replied, pulling mine off. "Because I'm never putting mine on again."

There was ketchup all over it.

AT LEAST IT'S NOT BUBBLE GUM, BABYMOUSE.

Not-So-Secret Garden

For the next twenty minutes, we rehashed every single detail of our encounter: the brilliant choreography, the toe-tapping music—even the cleanliness of the bathrooms! The thing that finally broke the spell was honking from a nearby traffic jam.

I looked at my watch. It was already three p.m.! We had just two hours to find

Pizza Kitty's owner and get back to the museum. Luckily, we already knew where to find the next address on the list—1026 Peach Street—because it was the one we had missed earlier (when we took the subway the wrong way).

"This looks like a dead end," Penny said. We had come to a huge stone wall at the end of a street.

"Want to lift me up so I can see over the wall?" I asked.

"Sure," Penny said, placing Pizza Kitty down on the sidewalk.

After several unsuccessful attempts, she finally boosted me up far enough to see over the wall.

"What do you see?" Penny said, gasping under my weight.

"A park entrance right next to us!" I yelled. "And Pizza Kitty running away!"

"Oh no!" Penny shouted, catching me as I fell down. She grabbed the basket, and we ran into the park after Pizza Kitty.

It was a warm day, and people of all ages were out, soaking up the sun. They were playing sports, running, cycling, lounging— you name it!

We spotted Pizza Kitty easily from the commotion she was causing in the dog park. Penny and I tried to catch her, but she was scared of all the dogs and ran away every time we came near her.

Eventually, she ran up into a tree.

"How are we going to catch her?" Penny asked.

"I have an idea," I said, approaching a couple having a picnic.

"Are you done with that?" I asked them, pointing to their pizza box full of crusts.

They exchanged weird looks before the woman said, "Uh, sure."

"Thanks!" I said, scooping it up.

I ran into the dog park.

"Excuse me! Pardon me!" I said, pushing through the crowd. "Pizza delivery!" I put the box on the ground underneath the tree and waited.

At first, nothing happened. But slowly, Pizza Kitty climbed down through the branches, and she leaped into the pizza box.

"You did it!" Penny cried. "She really is Pizza Kitty after all."

Penny and I gently put her back in my

basket (along with the crusts). A group of onlookers began to clap and cheer, and I couldn't help but smile. Penny snapped a photo on my camera.

Exhausted, we tossed the pizza box into a recycling bin and found an empty bench to collapse on. Penny and I sat for a minute, taking in the scene. That was the first time I noticed there were super-cute pigeons everywhere!

"Aww," I said to Penny. "I wish I had something I could feed these pigeons. . . ."

"How about the crusts?" Penny asked, reaching into the basket.

Pizza Kitty meowed ferociously.

"Okay, maybe not," said Penny, pulling back her hand. "Oh, we have the leftover dumplings from lunch!" She pulled out the doggy bag.

"Perfect!" I said, ripping it open.

"Uh, Babymouse," Penny warned. "I don't think you should do that. . . ."

But it was too late. Swarms of pigeons descended on me all at once.

Well, I learned my lesson.

After I brushed the feathers off, we hit the road once more.

I thought it would be easy to get from one side of the park to the other, but in reality, it was like a windy maze with no easy starting or ending point.

The paths all looked like straight lines, but then they would unexpectedly veer off to one side or back the other way. Plus, it was hilly, so you couldn't see far in any direction.

Suddenly, we came to a fork in the road. "Let's go this way," Penny said, pointing to the left.

"Really? I feel like we should go that way," I said, pointing right.

We decided to climb the huge boulder in front of us to get a better view.

From the top of the boulder, we could see very far in all directions. Soon, we were on the right track again, nearing the park exit, when something flew past me.

SWOOSH!

I looked up to see a soccer ball bounce off the park fence and roll right in front of me.

"Hey, kid!" a voice called.

I turned around. A professional-looking soccer player was standing there, the rest of her team in the background.

"Kick it!" she shouted.

I immediately started to panic. It was just like I was back in gym class.

"Go for it, Babymouse!" Penny said, cheering me on.

Top of the World, Baby!

fter the soccer ball fiasco, I was glad to be out of that park!

And even more so when we saw the information stand near the exit. I was thrilled to see it had tons of maps of the city.

I'd never realized how much I relied on my Whiz Bang™ to get around. Using a real paper map was pretty old-fashioned, but it was also kind of cool.

"May I have one map, please?" I asked a man who was working there.

"Sure," he replied, showing me samples. "The laminated ones are $6.75, and the paper ones are $3.50. Plus tax."

"Oh—uh," I stammered. "Are any of them free?"

"Free?" The man laughed, nudging his partner. "Sorry, kid!"

"Psst! Babymouse!" Penny whispered.

"What?"

She pointed to a trash can. "I'm pretty sure I just saw someone throw out a map!"

We rushed over and peered into the trash can. Sure enough, near the bottom was a map.

Huzzah!

Neither of us wanted to stick our hand in there, so we decided to flip a coin. But we were so broke we didn't even have a coin to toss! We ended up using a bottle cap we found on the ground instead.

I lost the flip (of course), which meant Penny would get to hold Pizza Kitty while I dug around for someone's old map in the trash.

"If only I had a glove or something," I said, holding my nose and putting my arm into the toxic can. Then I remembered—I did have a glove, the one Tommy H had given me!

I reached into my bag and pulled it on.

We arrived at 1026 Peach Street about fifteen minutes later. It was an old brick apartment building, six floors high. Penny and I peered into the courtyard before deciding the coast was clear of dogs. (I had sure learned that lesson!)

"Hmmm. Was there an apartment number listed?" I asked Penny.

She frowned. "Nope. Just the street address."

"You can't be serious!" I groaned. "What now?!"

"I guess we'll have to try every door," she said.

We both sighed. This was going to take some time. I looked at the long shadows in the courtyard. The sun was already starting to go down. We had to hurry!

We climbed the stairs to the door. I tugged on the handle a few times, but the door didn't open.

Penny got behind me, and she pulled me as I pulled the door.

Still nothing.

"How do we get in this place?" I asked.

"Maybe we have to press one of these buttons," Penny suggested, pointing to a panel of buttons with numbers.

I started pressing every button.

Silence. Then, suddenly, a bunch of different voices began coming through the intercom.

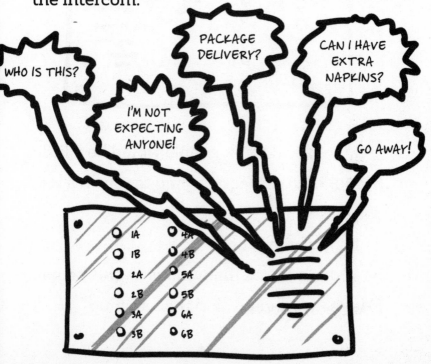

I looked at Penny and stammered, "Uh—
I have a lost cat here."

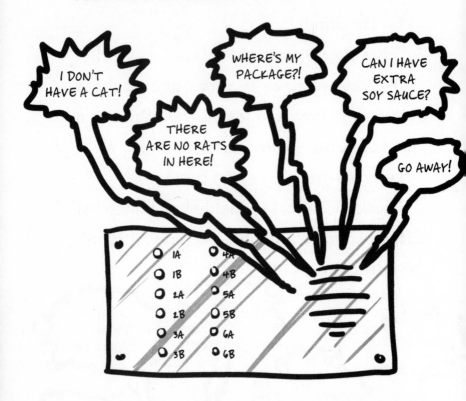

Man. You'd think people would be a little
friendlier to someone trying to return a lost
cat!

Penny bit her lip.

"I don't know, Babymouse," she began.
"Maybe we should skip this building."

"But what if this is Pizza Kitty's home?" I said, holding up the kitten. "Pizza Kitty, do you live here?"

Pizza Kitty blinked.

"Maybe she can give us a hint," Penny suggested. "Let's put her on the stoop and see what she does."

That was a great idea!

We gently placed Pizza Kitty on the ground and watched her closely.

She licked her fur.

"Maybe she's trying to say something to us in secret code," Penny said doubtfully.

"Like we'll be looking fur-ever?" I asked.

Pizza Kitty curled up in a ball and closed her eyes.

"What a cute kitten!" a voice behind us announced.

We turned to see a girl about our age with a backpack, walking up the stairs. She must have been coming home from school.

"Is she yours?" the girl asked.

"No," Penny replied. "But is she yours?"

The girl looked puzzled.

"She's lost. We're trying to find her owner," I explained.

"Ah," said the girl. "Well, I can let you in, but I can't help you look. I have a ton of homework tonight." She dumped her bag on the top step with a **PLOP** and pulled out her key.

"Great—thanks!" I said, putting Pizza Kitty back in the basket.

Getting into the building seemed like a win, but then I remembered how many apartments we still had to visit. . . .

I knocked on the first door.

A woman in hair curlers peeked through a small opening.

"Hello," I said with a smile. "We're here to see if—"

"Oh, hold on. Just let me get my checkbook," she said, and disappeared before we could stop her.

"Checkbook?" mouthed Penny.

I shrugged.

In a minute, she was back.

"Okay, yes, I would like three boxes of Dark Chocolateys, two boxes of Raspberry Razzies, and one box of Lemon Lemonies. How much will that be?"

"Oh, uh, actually, we're just here to see if this is your lost kitten," I said, holding up my basket.

"Oh no, never! I'm horribly allergic to cats! I thought you were selling Animal Scout cookies."

She shut the door in our faces.

☆ ♡ ☆

It didn't get much better from there.

By the time we got to the top floor, Penny and I were completely wiped out. We plodded along until we got to the very last apartment door. I was too tired to knock, so I just let my head fall forward into the door with a **clunk.**

"Coming!" a voice yelled from inside. When the door opened, we were surprised to see it was the girl who had let us in.

"Oh, hey, it's you two!" she said. "Any luck?"

We shook our heads sadly. Pizza Kitty let out a disheartened **meow.**

"Bummer," she said. "But since you're already up here, want to see something cool?"

My whiskers perked up.

"Sure!" Penny and I said at the same time.

The girl led us toward a heavy door in the hallway outside her apartment.

"My name's Glinda," she said.

"Did you say Glinda?" I asked, eyes wide.

"No, **Linda**," she corrected me.

"Oh." I tried to hide my disappointment.

"I'm Penny," said Penny.

"And I'm Babymouse," I added. "And this is Pizza Kitty."

"Nice to meet you, Pizza Kitty," said Linda, jokingly shaking the kitten's tiny paw.

We stepped through the door and walked up a small flight of steps onto a large concrete deck. We were on the roof!

"Wow!" Penny exclaimed, holding Pizza Kitty safely in the basket.

From there, we could see the WHOLE CITY! It was the most incredible thing I had ever seen. The sun setting over the buildings left a pretty pink-and-orange glow. You could almost taste the cotton candy clouds. I felt like Dorothy seeing the Emerald City for the first time.

"Now, **that's** what I call a masterpiece," I said. I took out my camera and snapped a picture.

"You can see on and on forever!" Penny exclaimed.

"Yeah," said Linda proudly. "I love this view. It never gets old."

"Almost makes knocking on every door in the building feel worth it," Penny said quietly.

"**Almost**," I emphasized.

"Yeah," Linda said. "It's too bad you didn't find the owner. But I'm not surprised because our landlord doesn't allow pets in the building."

Penny and I exchanged glances that said, "**Now** you tell us?!"

Suddenly, a clock on a nearby tower began to ring.

"It's four o'clock!" Penny and I shouted.

"We've got to go now, or we'll miss the bus home," I said, heading for the door.

"Bye! Thanks for showing us your roof!" Penny yelled to Linda.

"No prob!" Linda said, waving us off. "Good luck with everything!"

Last Bus to School

Back on the street, we consulted our
list of street names:

Paxton P...
~~Peach Street~~ e
~~Peacock Street~~
Peanut Street
~~Pearl Street~~
...bble Terrace

There was only one place left: Peanut Street. I remembered from the soda-soaked map that it was not far from the museum, so we decided to make our way back in that direction. We were still about thirty blocks north.

My flip-flops weren't exactly made for running, but there was no time to waste. We couldn't stop for food, water, the bathroom, or anything in the world other than—

"KAZOO!" Penny exclaimed.

"What?" I asked, shocked.

"Kazoo! This is the store Felicia and her friends were talking about on the bus!"

Penny was right! I definitely remembered them talking about Kazoo as the hottest boutique in the city.

"We have to stop!" I announced.

"But we don't have any time to check it out," Penny said sadly.

I thought fast.

"What if we just run in, look around, and then leave without buying anything?" I asked.

"I don't know," Penny said, looking at Pizza Kitty.

"We can run extra fast on the way back," I begged with a pleading smile.

"Okay, okay," she agreed. "But no trying on!"

"Yes!" I exclaimed.

We hurried into the store excitedly, but immediately stopped and looked around, confused. The store was full of . . . **kazoos**?!?!

"Welcome to Kazoo!" said a sales associate. "**The** hottest new pop-up kazoo store in the city." He blew into a kazoo, making a loud whizzing noise, then handed us stickers with kazoos on them.

"Huh?" I asked. "Where are the clothes?"

"Oh, you're thinking of **Kazu**, the cloth-ing store," he said, nodding. "That's on the other side of town."

Le sigh.

Penny pointed to the clock.

"We only have thirty minutes left to get to the City Museum!" she reminded me.

"Sounds like you're in a rush!" the salesman said. "Why don't you take one of our Ka-Zoom promotional vehicles behind the store. Just show the driver the sticker I gave you, and they'll take you anywhere you want to go. It's part of a new ad campaign directed at—"

But we had no time to listen to his pitch.

"Thanks!" I yelled as we ran into the alley behind the store and saw a fleet of small pedicabs with the Ka-Zoom logo.

We waved to the first driver we saw— who was kind of hard to miss.

He was dressed like a . . . wait for it . . . **kazoo.**

It was definitely attention-grabbing. I mean, it's not every day you see someone in a kazoo costume pedaling down the street.

"Not another costumed character," I whispered to Penny.

She laughed and showed him her sticker.

"Can you please take us to the City Museum as quickly as possible?" I asked.

"Sure thing!" he said. "Buckle up! It's gonna be a funky ride."

A funky ride? Was that good or bad? Penny and I looked at each other, confused.

But as soon as the vehicle started, we understood why. A symphony of kazoos began pounding through the sound system.

We covered our ears, and Pizza Kitty pulled the top of my basket closed.

After what felt like an eternity, the Ka-Zoom stopped.

"This is as far as I'm allowed to go," he said. "City noise-pollution ordinance."

"Okay, we'll get out here. Thanks!" I said. It was ten minutes till five p.m.

Penny and I got out and began to run toward the museum. We frantically counted the minutes as we went.

4:52...

4:53...

4:54...

4:55...

4:56...

Finally, we were just one block away. I was running so fast that I completely lost one of my flip-flops.

"Nooo!" I yelled.

In what felt like slow motion, I turned to grab my flip-flop. As I did so, I noticed the name of the street we were crossing.

"Peanut Street!" I shouted.

Pizza Kitty popped her head out of the basket and sniffed the air.

"This is your street, right, girl?" I asked her.

"Meow!" she meowed.

4:57...

There were rows of fancy brownstones on both sides of the street. I looked back for Penny, who was half a block behind me.

She was waving me on. "Go! Go!" she yelled.

4:58...

Finally, I made it to 1026 Peanut Street. This brownstone was identical to the others, except it had several colorful flowerpots in the entryway and a welcome mat that read "Meow." This HAD to be the place.

If it wasn't, Pizza Kitty would be heading home with me. Maybe my parents would let me keep her? She was way cuter than my

little brother and probably not as annoying.

4:59 . . .

Penny met me near the end of the block. We turned and ran back toward the museum.

"Did you find it?!" she asked, looking at my empty basket.

"Yes," I said, gasping for air. "Her owner was thrilled."

"Aw," said Penny. "I'm glad she's finally home."

☆ ♥ ☆

We got to the bus with seconds to spare. Ms. Painter was talking with the bus driver. Our classmates had just started forming a line by the door. Wilson and Georgie waved us over.

"Man, what happened to you two?" Wilson asked. I guess we were looking a little rough after our all-day adventure.

"It's kind of a long story," I told him.

"Check out the postcards I got," he said, holding them out. It was then I remembered my art collection!

"Ms. Painter, I left something at the coat check!" I cried.

"Okay," she said. "But please hurry. We really need to get going."

I nodded and dashed into the building as fast as I could.

Of course, there was a long line at the coat check. (Was there a line for everything in this city?!) I waited impatiently as it dwindled down. Finally, it was my turn, and I thrust my number at the man behind the counter. He went to the back to locate my cubby, and after what felt like the longest ten seconds of my life, he reappeared with my tube in hand.

"Thanks!" I said, taking it like a baton in a relay race. I ran to the bus as fast as my feet could carry me.

When I finally got onto the bus, a horrible fishy smell hit my nose.

"What's that smell?"

"Some kid left their tuna fish sandwich on the bus all day," the driver grumbled.

Eek.

I slid into a seat next to Penny. But even the terrible smell couldn't take the shine off my day. What an adventure!

I missed Pizza Kitty already.

I reached into my pocket and pulled out the list. I crossed off "Peanut Street" and drew a little heart next to it.

Penny patted me on the shoulder. I could tell she felt the same way.

Ms. Painter walked up and down the aisle, counting students.

"Hmm," she said. "Looks like we're four students short. . . ."

Just then, I heard yelling coming from outside. I looked out the window to see Felicia, Melinda, Belinda, and Berry running toward the bus. Their arms were full of shopping bags.

"I guess Kazu doesn't have its own Ka-Zums," Penny said with a smirk.

There's No Place Like School

We got back to the school late, so there were no buses to take us home. Luckily, Mom came right on time. I hopped in and buckled up.

"Hey, Babymouse!" she said. "How was the big day?"

I thought of sweet Pizza Kitty.

I thought of my sore feet.

I thought of my poor broken Whiz

Bang™ sitting in my basket and wondered what to say.

I thought for a moment.

"Penny and I had a great time exploring. We saw a lot of beautiful things."

"That's great!" Mom said. "What was the best part of the museum?"

I paused to think again.

"You know, I really liked the gift shop!" I replied truthfully.

"The gift shop, huh?" Mom mused. "I was wondering about those flip-flops. Well, as long as you enjoyed yourself!"

"I really did," I said with a smile.

☆ ♥ ☆

When we got home, I collapsed onto a kitchen chair.

Dad had saved me a plate of leftovers. It was . . . pizza.

Pizza Kitty.

>sniff<

After that, I was ready to call it a day. I showered, brushed my teeth and whiskers, put on my softest pajamas, and climbed into bed.

I smiled up at my Tommy H poster. (I knew I recognized that grin from somewhere!)

I was about to set my phone alarm, but then I remembered that my phone was completely shattered. Argh. I thought about all the warnings my parents had given me when I first got my Whiz Bang™. Maybe I would wait a little to tell them what hap-

pened (seeing as how I'd broken the first one not too long ago . . .).

I set the alarm on the digital clock on my nightstand. Then I immediately fell asleep.

When I got back to school the next day, I was actually happy to see Locker. I decorated it with the trinkets from my adventures with Penny.

Just then, I saw Felicia, Melinda, Belinda, and Berry coming out of the principal's office. They did **not** look happy.

"I can't believe we got a week's worth of detention!" Felicia growled.

"And we didn't even get to eat at the sushi place!" Melinda wailed. "Who knew we needed reservations?"

"Ugh," Belinda said. "And no matinee show for **Koalaton**! What gives?"

"I know!" Berry groaned. "We have the worst luck in the world."

I smiled but said nothing as they went by. Penny and I had decided to keep our little adventure a secret (from everyone but Wilson and Georgie, that is).

The day passed by painfully slowly. My legs were aching from all the walking we did the day before. My feet were still sore, too.

And for the first time ever, I was dreading art class. What if Ms. Painter asked us questions about the museum?!

Luckily, my friends helped me calm down.

"What's the worst that can happen?" Wilson asked during lunch. "They give you detention?"

"Yeah, that's not so bad," Georgie said. "Except you'd get stuck with Felicia and her friends all week. Ugh!"

I hadn't thought of that. If I did end up with detention, I would **technically** get to hang out with the popular girls for a whole five days. . . .

But no. I didn't think even that would be worth it.

The bell rang. Time for art class.

When we walked into the room, we saw Ms. Painter holding a stack of papers.

"Oh no!" I whispered to Penny. "What do you think it could be?"

She met my eyes nervously. "I hope it's not a pop quiz."

"She's probably going to make me write out my last will and testament," I whispered.

BEING OF SOUND MIND AND WHISKERS, I, BABYMOUSE, DO HEREBY BEQUEATH TO SQUEAK ALL THE HOT WATER IN THE BATHROOM, THE FRONT SEAT OF THE CAR, THE BIGGER BEDROOM, AND MY BROKEN-BEYOND-REPAIR WHIZ BANG™. I BEQUEATH TO PENNY MY TOMMY H GLOVE AND ALL TOMMY H MEMORABILIA.

SIGNED, BABYMOUSE

WHAT ABOUT ME, BABYMOUSE?

"Okay, students," Ms. Painter said. "Please take your seats."

The chatter died down as everyone settled in and took out their supplies. The room got so quiet I could hear my heart beating.

"Obviously, we had a very exciting day yesterday," she went on. "Some more exciting than others. . . ."

She shot a look at Felicia, Melinda, Belinda, and Berry.

I let out a loud **GULP.**

"I thought that today we could use our class time to reflect on art—all kinds of art—and what it means to us."

Georgie raised his hand, and Ms. Painter called on him.

"What do you mean by 'all kinds of art'?" he asked.

"Good question, Georgie," Ms. Painter said. "See, art isn't just about famous paintings in a museum. It can be different things to different people."

A lot of students looked confused.

Ms. Painter went on, "For example, to an architect, the museum itself could be considered a work of art. Or to an interior designer, the picture frames may be more interesting than what's inside them. There is no right or wrong way to explore or appreciate what inspires us. That's the beauty of art."

All kinds of art. I thought about that.

It was then I realized that while I didn't see a single piece of art in the museum, Penny and I had seen a lot of really beautiful art all over the city. It was ALL art, in a way.

Ms. Painter handed out sheets of paper, and I breathed a big sigh of relief. Things would be okay after all. I began to write and didn't stop until the bell rang.

I had written almost a whole page about art in the world, using the stuff we'd seen in the gift shop—the tote bags, umbrellas, scarves, and so on—as examples of how art can make people happy and help them express themselves.

On my way out of class, I put my essay in the pile on Ms. Painter's desk. That's when I noticed, on the corner of her desk, the limited-edition spoon from the gift shop!

"You got the spoon?!" I asked her excitedly.

"Yes," she said with a laugh. "I love that gift shop!"

"Me too!" I said. "That's actually what I wrote about!"

"Well, I'm really looking forward to reading your essay, Babymouse," Ms. Painter said.

I smiled. "See you tomorrow!"

"Oh, Babymouse," Ms. Painter said. "One more thing . . ."

I felt my stomach flip. Did she know the truth?

Was I going to get detention? What would my parents say? Between my cell phone and getting caught, I would be cleaning the house for the rest of my life!

I turned back around and was surprised to see her holding my poster tube.

"I found this on the bus yesterday," she said. "I didn't know who it belonged to, but when I looked inside, I saw your signed art-works. They're quite good! Would you be willing to let me hang them on the hallway bulletin board?"

My stomach flipped again, but in the best possible way.

"I would love that, Ms. Painter!" I said.

I couldn't believe it. My art was going to

end up on display after all! I walked out the door with a giant smile on my face.

THIS IS GIVING ME A LOT OF FEELS, BABYMOUSE.

What's more—it looked like I was offi-cially in the clear!

☆ ♥ ☆

The last day and a half had been such an emotional roller coaster. I thought back on everything that had happened. It had been more than just an adventure. It was a chance to see things and places I never even knew existed. I had grown up a lot in twenty-four hours.

Middle school sure was complicated. But at least it wasn't boring.

(Hmm, maybe I should use that in my next auditorium monologue. . . .)

I signed on to my computer to see that Penny was online.

We'd been planning our next trip to the city. Penny's mom said she would take us in for a day, and we had a list of places we wanted to visit. The theater, the dumpling

restaurant, and, of course, the house where
Pizza Kitty lived!

BIG CITY NEWSPAPER

TOP STORY

Kind Stranger Returns Missing Kitten and Declines $10,000 Reward!

"I have no idea who she was, but she sure had a big heart. And messy whiskers."

PUBLISHED 8:07 A.M. TODAY

A local retiree was willing to offer a fortune for the return of her favorite feline—but the Good

FEATURED

Babymouse ♡

Babymouse ♡

Babymouse ♡

ARTIST

Babymouse ♡

Babymouse ♡

Babymouse♡

Babymouse♡

Babymouse♡

About the Artist

Our class's featured artist, BABYMOUSSE, draws inspiration from many sources, including the theater, culinary arts, city scenes, and wildlife. The works shown here are from her "Cupcake Period," a phase of her artistic development that she admits may never truly be over.

☆ ♥ ☆

About the Authors

Jennifer L. Holm and **Matthew Holm** are a **New York Times** bestselling sister-and-brother team. They are the creators behind several popular series: Babymouse, Squish, The Evil Princess vs. the Brave Knight, and My First Comics. The Eisner Award–winning Babymouse books have introduced millions of children to graphic novels. Jennifer is also the **New York Times** bestselling author of **The Fourteenth Goldfish** and several other highly acclaimed novels, including three Newbery Honor winners: **Our Only May Amelia, Penny from Heaven,** and **Turtle in Paradise.** Matthew is also the author of **Marvin and the Moths** with Jonathan Follett.

New York Times bestselling authors of *Sunny Side Up*

JENNIFER L. HOLM & MATTHEW HOLM

BABYMOUSE

TALES FROM THE LOCKER

PRINCIPAL

Miss Communication

Babymouse has a smartphone, and she's not afraid to use it!